Welcome to Percy's Park!

Percy the park keeper
works hard looking after
the park and his animal
friends who live there.
But Percy still likes to
find time for some fun
and games. And, of
course, in Percy's Park,
there's always time
for a story…

The Rescue Party

First published in hardback in Great Britain by HarperCollins Publishers Ltd in 1993
First published in paperback by Picture Lions in 1994
New edition published by Collins Picture Books in 2003
This edition published by HarperCollins Children's Books in 2011

17 19 20 18 16

ISBN: 978-0-00-715516-3

Picture Lions and Collins Picture Books are imprints of the Children's Division,
part of HarperCollins Publishers Ltd.
HarperCollins Children's Books is a division of HarperCollins Publishers Ltd.

Text and illustrations copyright © Nick Butterworth 1993, 2011

The author/illustrator asserts the moral right to be identified
as the author/illustrator of the work.

Visit our website at: www.harpercollins.co.uk

Printed in China

Nick Butterworth

The Rescue Party

HarperCollins *Children's Books*

"What a perfect day for doing nothing," said Percy the park keeper.

Percy was having a day off.

He and some of his animal friends had brought a picnic to one of their favourite places in the park.

Percy took off his cap and made himself a sun hat by tying knots in the corners of his handkerchief. Then he propped himself against an old tree stump and opened his book.

The animals settled themselves around Percy and waited for tea.

It was warm in the sunshine and soon everyone began to doze. Suddenly they were disturbed by the sound of laughter.

Percy looked up. Three young rabbits, two brothers and their little sister, were playing a leaping game in the long grass. When they saw Percy, the rabbits waved.

"Hello Percy! We're pretending to be hares."

Percy chuckled and waved back as the rabbits went leaping away.

The three rabbits were having a wonderful time.

"I can jump the longest!" said one.

"I can run the fastest!" said his brother.

"I can jump the highest!" said the smallest rabbit and she jumped high into the air.

"Wheeeee!"

But as the little rabbit landed, to her brothers' surprise, she completely disappeared!

She had crashed right through the rotten cover of an old well.

The two brothers stared at the hole in the ground. Then they began to wail.

"Help! The ground has eaten our sister!"
"Help! Somebody help!"

Somebody, of course, meant Percy.

The two rabbits ran straight to him and told him what had happened.

The other animals looked worried as Percy listened and sighed.

"There's no water in that well," he said, "but it's very deep." He pulled on his cap and jumped to his feet.

"We'll need a rope," he said. "Come on."

Percy raced away with the animals following
behind him.

Before long he was leading them back again
towards the old well. Over his shoulder, Percy
carried a long rope.

Percy cleared away the rotten wood that had covered the well, and peered into the dark hole.

He couldn't see the little rabbit. She was perched on a log that had wedged itself halfway down the well.

"Helloooo," called Percy. "Can you hear me?"

A rather cross little voice answered.

"I bumped my head."

"But are you alright?" asked Percy.

"I bumped my head," answered the cross voice again.

"Hmm," said Percy, "I think she's alright."

"We're sending down a rope," called Percy. "Tie it nice and tight and we'll pull you up."

Percy lowered the rope into the well.

The little rabbit wasn't quite sure what to do, so she tied it tightly to the log that she was sitting on.

"Now, heave-ho!" said Percy.

Percy pulled on the rope, but nothing happened.
He pulled again.

"What's she been eating?" he muttered. "She weighs
a ton." He pulled once more, but still nothing
happened. Percy frowned.

"Alright," he said, "let's see what we can do
together."

D own in the well, the little rabbit was beginning to get used to the darkness. As she gazed around, she noticed that there was a small opening in the wall of the well.

"I wonder where that leads to," she said.

At the top of the well, the rescuers lined up behind Percy, ready to pull on the rope.

"Ready," shouted Percy. "Heave!"

Something in the well moved.

"Keep going," said Percy, "she's coming."

The rescuers pulled and pulled. They grunted and groaned and quacked and squeaked.

Up came the rope. But as it reached the top, the rescuers got a terrible surprise.

There was no little rabbit on the end of the
rope. All they had pulled up from the
well was a great big log!

"Well I'm blessed!" said Percy.

"What's happened to her?"

"She's turned into a log!" said the fox.
"She's at the bottom of the well!" said the squirrels.

"She's lost forever!" wailed the rabbits.

Percy and the animals began to laugh. They laughed and laughed until they couldn't stand up.

"But how did you manage to get out?" asked Percy at last.

"It was easy," she said. "I found a secret passage. It comes out just over there."

"Well I never!" said Percy. "Well, well, well. Which reminds me," he added, "I must make a new cover for that old well."

"Oh no I'm not," said a little voice behind them, "I'm here…"

Everyone looked round in amazement. There at the back of the line of rescuers was the little rabbit.

"I thought I'd help you," she said.

"What are we doing?"

"I'll do it tomorrow," said Percy as he led the
way back towards their picnic. "After all,"
he said, "today is my day off."

"I was born in London in 1946 and grew up in a sweet shop in Essex. For several years I worked as a graphic designer, but in 1980 I decided to concentrate on writing and illustrating books for children.

My wife, Annette, and I have two grown-up children, Ben and Amanda, and we have put down roots in the country.

I haven't recently counted how many books there are with my name on the cover but Percy the Park Keeper accounts for a good many of them. I'm reliably informed that they have sold in their millions, worldwide. Hooray!

I didn't realise this when I invented Percy, but I can now see that he's very like my mum's dad, my grandpa. Here's a picture of him giving a ride to my mum and my brother, Mike, in his old home-made wheelbarrow!"

Nick Butterworth

Nick Butterworth has presented children's stories on television, worked on a strip for *Sunday Express Magazine* and worked for various major graphic design companies. Among his books published by HarperCollins are *Thud!, QPootle5, Jingle Bells, Albert le Blanc, Tiger* and *The Whisperer*, which won the Nestlé Gold Award. But he is best known for his stories about Percy the Park Keeper who features on audio CD and DVD, as well as having appeared in his own television series.

Collect all the Percy the Park Keeper stories
OVER 8 MILLION BOOKS SOLD!

PB: 978-0-00-714693-2

PB: 978-0-00-715515-6

PB: 978-0-00-715516-3

PB: 978-0-00-715518-7

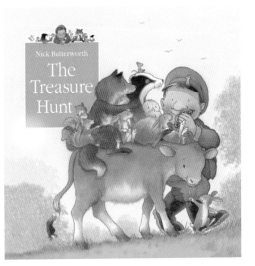

PB: 978-0-00-715517-0

PB: 978-0-00-715514-9

Percy the Park Keeper stories can be ordered at:

www.harpercollins.co.uk